Robin
and
Maid Marian

by Damian Harvey and Martin Remphry

FRANKLIN WATTS
LONDON•SYDNEY

First published in 2009 by
Franklin Watts
338 Euston Road
London
NW1 3BH

Franklin Watts Australia
Level 17/207 Kent Street
Sydney
NSW 2000

A CIP catalogue record for this book is available
from the British Library.

ISBN 978 0 7496 8556 0 (hbk)
ISBN 978 0 7496 8567 6 (pbk)

Series Editor: Jackie Hamley
Series Advisor: Dr Barrie Wade
Series Designer: Peter Scoulding

Printed in China

Franklin Watts is a division of
Hachette Children's Books,
an Hachette UK company
www.hachette.co.uk

It was a beautiful summer's day in
Sherwood Forest, but Robin Hood
was feeling very miserable.

"What's the matter with Robin?" asked Much the Miller's son. "He's in love with Maid Marian," said Little John. "They haven't seen each other since he came to Sherwood Forest."

"I'm going to see her," Robin said.
"Just to make sure she's safe."

"You can't do that," said Little John. "If you go near the castle, the Sheriff's soldiers will throw you in prison."

"You could go in disguise,"
said Much, "then no one
will recognise you."
"That's a great idea!" cried Robin.

7

Robin put on one of Friar Tuck's
old robes and wrapped a scarf
round his face. "Even my friends
won't recognise me now,"
laughed Robin Hood.

But Little John still wasn't happy. "I've heard there's a swordsman who is hunting for you in the forest," he said. "What if he captures you?"

"He won't capture me!" said
Robin. "I can fight any man!
And anyway, if I get into trouble
I can blow my horn."

Robin waved to his friends, then disappeared into Sherwood Forest.

Robin hadn't gone far when he met a stranger walking through the forest. "What are you doing in my forest?" asked Robin Hood.

"This is not your forest," said the
stranger. "And, if you must know,
I'm looking for Robin Hood."
Robin drew his sword. "Then you
must first get past me," he said.

The stranger's sword flashed brightly and clanged against Robin's sword. "Ah ha!" said Robin. "Is that the best you can do?"

The stranger jumped, and kicked
Robin over with one foot.

Robin fell into some mud
and dropped his sword.

As quickly as he could, Robin
jumped to his feet and picked up
his sword. But the stranger was
even quicker, and Robin's sword
was sent flying through the air.

Robin drew his bow, but the stranger chopped it in half before he could reach for an arrow.

"You are a fine fighter,"
said Robin. "That's enough!"
"Good!" said the stranger. "Now tell
me where I can find Robin Hood."

Robin took out his horn and
blew it as loudly as he could.
"You have already found Robin
Hood," said Robin. "And now
you will meet my merry men."

Little John, Will Scarlett and all of Robin's merry men surrounded the stranger. "Drop your sword," shouted Little John, "or you will be sorry you met us today!"

The stranger's sword fell to the floor and Robin frowned.

"Now show yourself," he said, "so we can all see the man that beat Robin Hood."

21

The stranger took off the black robes and the merry men were amazed. "He's wearing a dress!" said Little John.

23

Then the stranger took off the
black hat and the merry men
could not believe their eyes.
"It's a girl!" said Much. "Robin had
his bow chopped in half by a girl!"

Robin took off his own disguise and laughed. "This is not just any girl," he said. "This is Maid Marian. I didn't recognise her in that disguise."

"And I didn't recognise you,"
said Maid Marian. "I hope
I didn't hurt you."

"I'm glad you can take care of
yourself," said Robin. "But you
did break my favourite bow."

Little John and the merry men laughed and cheered. Then they lifted Maid Marian and Robin Hood onto their shoulders.

"Come on," said Little John. "We have a special guest for supper. Let's go home before Friar Tuck eats all the food!"

Puzzle 1

Put these pictures in the correct order.
Which event do you think is most important?
Now try writing the story in your own words!

Puzzle 2

Choose the correct speech bubbles for each
character. Can you think of any others?
Turn over to find the answers.

Answers

Puzzle 1

The correct order is: 1f, 2a, 3e, 4b, 5c, 6d

Puzzle 2

Maid Marian: 2, 3

Robin Hood: 1, 6

Little John: 4, 5

Look out for more Hopscotch Adventures:

TALES OF KING ARTHUR

1. The **Sword in the Stone**
ISBN 978 0 7496 6694 1

2. **Arthur the King**
ISBN 978 0 7496 6695 8

3. The **Round Table**
ISBN 978 0 7496 6697 2

4. **Sir Lancelot** and the **Ice Castle**
ISBN 978 0 7496 6698 9

5. **Sir Gawain** and the **Green Knight**
ISBN 978 0 7496 8557 7*
ISBN 978 0 7496 8569 0

6. **Sir Galahad** and the **Holy Grail**
ISBN 978 0 7496 8558 4*
ISBN 978 0 7496 8570 6

TALES OF ROBIN HOOD

Robin and the **Knight**
ISBN 978 0 7496 6699 6

Robin and the **Monk**
ISBN 978 0 7496 6700 9

Robin and the **Silver Arrow**
ISBN 978 0 7496 6703 0

Robin and the **Friar**
ISBN 978 0 7496 6702 3

Robin and the **Butcher**
ISBN 978 0 7496 8555 3*
ISBN 978 0 7496 8568 3

Robin and **Maid Marian**
ISBN 978 0 7496 8556 0*
ISBN 978 0 7496 8567 6

TALES OF SINBAD THE SAILOR

Sinbad and the **Ogre**
ISBN 978 0 7496 8559 1*
ISBN 978 0 7496 8571 3

Sinbad and the **Whale**
ISBN 978 0 7496 8553 9*
ISBN 978 0 7496 8565 2

Sinbad and the **Diamond Valley**
ISBN 978 0 7496 8554 6*
ISBN 978 0 7496 8566 9

Sinbad and the **Monkeys**
ISBN 978 0 7496 8560 7*
ISBN 978 0 7496 8572 0

For more *Hopscotch Adventures* and other *Hopscotch* stories, visit:
www.franklinwatts.co.uk

* hardback